Collected Alex **Winner**

2012 *Caketrain Chapbook Competition*

Michael Kimball, Final Judge

A L

EX

Collected Alex   A Novella by A.T. Grant

CAKETRAIN
[a journal and press]
Box 82588, Pittsburgh, Pennsylvania 15218
www.caketrain.org

Printed in the United States of America.
ISBN 978-0-988891 5-2-4

The Contents of Alex

I. The Body

The Dead Body at the Party

I could drag the dead body to the party. But the people. The people holding glasses of beer or wine or Diet Coke. The people having a good time. The people that would expect me to have a good time. They would expect me to make conversation and not worry about the body. The body that I have been dragging around for years and years. The body that is leaking and rotting and beginning to smell the way a leaking, rotting dead body smells. Maybe they would be able to tell from the smell that I have not been taking care of it. That I am performing an experiment. That I have not been feeding the body its special formula. They would notice the scribbled hair, the wrecked fingernails, the trail of goo that leaks from all of its holes. And they would try to start a conversation. They would say:

That's *some* dead body.

How long have you had that thing.

And where do you get something like that anyway.

Do they come with instructions.

What's the rate of decomposition.

Do you ever—you know.

Did you get it because of that movie. What was it called.

It must make a great punching bag.

It's been *how* many days since you've given the body its special formula.

Then they would address the body directly. Ask if it isn't tired of being dragged around by *this guy* all the time as they jerk their thumbs in my direction. He's such a character, they would laugh. And they would put a drink in the body's hand and pose it like it was flirting with a group of women. And they would take photos of the body and me with their iPhones. And then there would be a tagged photo of the body and me on Facebook the next morning. The tags would read: — with The Body and Alex.

I could drag the body to the party. I could lug the body downstairs from my apartment and into the car. I could strap the body in, start the car and drive. But we don't go to the party. We don't really go anywhere.

The Day They Gave Me the Dead Body

My eighth birthday was when my parents gave me this dead body.

Go ahead, my mother said. It won't bite.

My parents held each other and watched as I inspected it. They were so excited. My mother bit her lip. I lifted the dead body's arm by the wrist. Its skin was smooth and felt like it might burst if I gave it a sharp poke. When I let go, its hand smacked against the hardwood. I stuck my finger between its third and fourth ribs. One of them felt broken. I sat for a moment on its chest. No movement. I opened its mouth to look at its teeth. A bad smell came out of the mouth, so I closed it. I opened its eyelids. The eyes were little black discs with nothing behind them.

How do you play with it, I asked.

Well, you don't *play* with it, exactly.

Oh, I said. I looked up and down the body again, then rolled it over. What am I supposed to do with it.

Pick it up, my father said. He picked up the body and threw it over his right shoulder. Like this, he said. Carry it around awhile, see how it feels.

So I did.

The body was much larger than me, probably twice my size. I staggered under its weight. It looked like it was about twenty-five years old when it died.

Once I got it balanced on my shoulder I asked, How long has it been dead.

They did not answer. My mother got the camera, while my father beamed at me, the body draped over my shoulder. They looked so proud. I placed the body on the floor as gently as I could. I looked into its face. My mother raised the camera. I heard the flash begin to charge.

How did it die, I asked, still looking into the body's face.

The camera snapped, flashed.

The Experiment

A few weeks ago I decided to stop giving the body its formula. I wondered if I would still be able to carry the body around. I wondered if the body would break into pieces or turn inside out or dissolve completely. I wondered if I would feel guilt about destroying the dead body that had been given to me, or if someone, I don't know who, the Dead Body Protective Care Service if such a thing exists, would come and take the body away from me.

When I had the idea, it felt like a hole opened in my head. I am not sure where the idea came from. But it came. Maybe I saw a farmer carry a feedsack over his shoulder, then heave it into the back of his truck and dust off his hands. Maybe I saw a couple on television break up, their bodies stiff on the screen. Maybe it had been a particularly long day of carrying the body around. Maybe I was just tired.

Wherever You Go

Always keep your dead body close, my parents told me. Never let it out of your sight.

But, I said, but it's so heavy.

It will make you stronger, my mother said. I looked at the floor, but she lifted my chin so our eyes met. You can do it. You have to try. For us.

So I began carrying it everywhere. First I practiced carrying it around my room. I learned how to avoid the corners of my bed, my desk. I learned to raise the body up so its feet would not drag.

Careful, my parents would say when I raised it too near the fan or when I went through a doorframe. You don't want to knock it in the head.

I looked at its head, swollen with lumps.

Okay, I said.

Once I could carry it safely around my room, I practiced carrying it back and forth through the house. I learned all of the trouble spots of the indoors. Sometimes my parents gave me lessons for particular spots—

Take the stairs one at a time.

Be careful not to let the hair dangle into the lit stovetop.

Don't let the body rest too close to the fireplace or an ember might jump onto its clothes.

Same goes for the space heater.

Be sure the arms and legs don't flop and knock over the ironing board.

Be careful not to slip and drop the body when you take it out of the bathtub.

—and so on.

I carried it for hours each day. When one shoulder got tired, I switched the body to the other. When both shoulders got tired, I set it against a wall. The dead body made a good cushion. I leaned against it and used its legs as armrests.

After a few months, my carrying was good enough to take the body outside of the house.

Stares

At first it was difficult to get used to the stares. I was the only kid on the block that carried a body around. I knew that all eyes were on the body, and because I carried it, I knew that all the people who looked at the body saw me, but only out of the corners of their eyes, pale and out of focus. Sometimes I felt the need to compete with the body for attention. I tried wearing a bright red shirt. I tried wearing a very tall blaze orange hat. I tried walking with a limp. I tried shouting everywhere I went. No matter what I did, I never felt the attention clot directly onto me as I carried the body down the street.

Even at home, I felt like my parents always looked at some neutral point between the dead body and me. Every picture was: the body and Alex playing mini-golf, the body and Alex at the beach, the body and Alex – Christmas '95. And when they said anything to me, they made sure to also reference the body somehow: Did you have a good day at school. Did the body stay propped up the entire time. It was as if they were afraid of showing favoritism.

Once when my family was at the city park, I laid the body flat on the grass and covered it with a pile of leaves. Then I lay down on top of the pile. Where did the dead body go, I said. Looks like I'm the only one here.

Later I began to enjoy the soft focus. I carried the body up and down the street for hours. I wore dull gray clothes so that I could feel myself dissolve into the background, into the warm and grainy feeling.

Routine

After a few months of lugging the dead body everywhere I went, we began to settle into a routine.

Every morning I helped the body out of its sleeping bag. I stretched the dead body's arms high over its head, then I opened its mouth and I yawned. I set the body in the corner while I made up my bed, then I used its arms and hands to roll up its sleeping bag and stash it under my bed.

Then we went into the bathroom. I cleaned the crust out of my eyes, then its eyes. I propped the body on the toilet while I showered, but it never had to pee or anything. Then while I peed I let the body soak in the bath. The body always left a thick oily film on the water's surface. My parents gave me special soaps to use on the body after it had soaked for several minutes. These will preserve the body, my father said. We want it to last for a long time, don't we.

After I brushed our teeth and combed our hair, I worked each of the body's joints. You have to work its joints every day, mother said. If you don't it will stiffen up and become difficult to carry and store in different positions.

She told me I should also stretch and flex its muscles each morning. These are the things that make a body last, she said. It's just as important to keep a dead body in shape as it is to keep a live body in shape.

When we finished our morning workout, we went downstairs for breakfast. My parents would give me cereal with marshmallows. To the body they gave a teaspoon of a special liquid formula. It was thick, and it took a long time to drip down the body's throat. I imagined it sliding, sliding, sliding down into the belly.

Once I asked if I could taste the special liquid formula. You have your cereal, my mother said. Eat up.

I just want to try it. What happens if you put it in a live body.

Son, my father said. The formula isn't made for a live body. Bad things would happen. He put his hand on the back of my neck. Promise your mother and me right now that you won't ever taste the formula. That you'll only feed it to the body.

I shook my head yes and said, I promise.

Besides, that stuff can't taste good. My father squinched his face, then smiled and patted me on the head. Better go. You don't want to be late for school.

My mother screwed the cap onto the bottle of formula and put it on the top shelf. I kissed my mother and father like always. Then I puckered the body's lips and made it give my parents each a kiss too.

I still wondered what the special formula tasted like, but I never asked about it again.

Recess

At recess the kids made up songs about me and the dead body. One of them went: *Alex and the body / flush them down the potty / dead ones, dead ones / they both fall down*

After the kids sang the song, they would poke the body, then scatter across the playground, holding their noses. Then they would make *P. U.* and *yuck* faces. They would squeal and giggle.

Then I would haul the body up the tallest slide and sit there for awhile. We would watch the other children climb on the monkey bars and pretend the old tires were a fort. We would watch them play freeze tag and hide-and-go-seek.

Don't you wish we could run, I said to the body one time.

When we got tired of watching, sometimes I let the body slide first so it could cushion me when I landed. Other times I slid first with the body right behind me for extra momentum.

The teacher always noticed after one or two slides.

Alex, she would say. We're happy to let you bring your dead body to school, but we can't let you take it onto the playground equipment. It will make a mess, and that wouldn't be fair to the other children, would it.

I guess not.

Now, she would say with a smile, there are plenty of places where you and the dead body can play. Run along and have fun.

The body and I always ended up making mounds in the dirt pile, humming.

A Chest of Drawers

Sometimes the dead body gets so heavy.

Sometimes I get tired of carrying it on my shoulders, so I drag it and its mouth fills up with mud and leaves. And for some reason it is more bloated at certain times than at others. It must be humidity or something. Or maybe its dead organs are swelling.

When it gets so heavy, I wish the dead body were a chest of drawers. I could pull out some drawers to lighten the load.

Once I tried cutting off one of its legs. It made the body a little bit lighter, but then a few hours later when I was ready to reattach the leg, I had trouble finding it. Then once I found the leg, I couldn't slide it back into joint. We had to take the body to a doctor.

Well, the doctor said, I'm afraid I've got bad news: the patient is dead. He laughed and clapped me on the back. Cheer up, son, he said. We can fix the leg.

Hours later, we left with the leg reattached and cherry suckers for the body and me, which neither of us ate. My parents didn't say anything, but I could tell they were upset by the quiet of the car ride home, by the way they touched my head as they tucked me into bed that night.

I felt awful. Maybe I should just take the organs out, I thought. Then I could use the body as a bag. I could open it up and crawl inside.

The Woods

I pick up the body and hoist it over my shoulder. My shoulder is sore from carrying the body yesterday to the grocery store and then around the shopping mall, where I bought some new boots, and then all around the parking lot when I forgot where we parked. So I switch the body to my other shoulder and begin walking into the woods.

The woods are where the body and I feel the best. All of that quiet and no expectations. No walls or other people. We can be the dead body and the guy who carries the dead body. And if we walk for long enough, we always find a dead tree that is held up by some living trees.

The ground is still wet from the rain and mist this morning. Water drips from the leaves onto the body which then drips onto me. My new boots are heavy. These are by far the deepest footprints we have ever made, I say to the body. I take a step and watch my foot sink deep into the mud, then I watch the print fill up with water as my foot leaves the depression.

Depression is a word I've never heard my mother use. I wonder if she ever used it once in her entire life. I think the closest she ever came was years ago on my graduation night. She was driving us to a "surprise" graduation party. The body and I were strapped into the back seat as usual, but I kept catching my mother's eye in the rear-view mirror.

What's wrong, I said.

Does it ever bother you to carry the body around all the time.

I can't imagine life without it, I said.

It's just that sometimes you seem a little down. She bit her lip. You know we are so proud of you.

I think when she said *bother* and *down* she meant *depression*. I would tell her now: it's not depression, it's just a dead body. I think she was afraid I couldn't handle it, carrying a dead thing around all the time.

Another time she said, Oh my son, what did we do to you.

When I find a rock in the woods, I prop the body against it and sit down. Its clothes are a little dirty. It has also been awhile since I have shaved the body's face. Or mine. I make a mental note: wash clothes, shave.

I wonder if the body's mother ever used the word *depression*. If the body's mother is still alive, maybe she is depressed right now.

Maybe when she dreams of the body, it is young and alive. In her dream, maybe she picks up the body after it has fallen asleep in front of the TV, carries it to its room, lays it in bed, tucks it in, pulls the covers all the way up to its chin, and puts a little glass of water on its nightstand.

Sometimes at night after I put the body into its sleeping bag, I run my hand through the body's hair. Its hair is very stiff. It almost feels fake. But I kiss its cold forehead anyway and smile like my parents used to do to me.

When I do, I hear the body's mother's voice, or at least what I imagine her voice sounds like, in my head. Goodnight sweetie, she says. The body's mother sounds just like my mother. I hear their voices blend. Goodnight sweetie, they say to both of us.

Most Nights

On the nights when we do not go to the park or drive around aimlessly, the dead body and I stay in and watch a movie or a boxing match. Sometimes we put on special headgear and box with each other, or I have a bowl of cereal while I feed the body its special formula, or I put the body on the couch and I sit in the chair farthest away.

From that distance, the body almost looks alive in the blue light, like it is very bored or sleeping but not dead, not gone. This is when the distance between us is greatest. The dead body across the room, with me imagining the body is alive. But it is also the closest we ever get to being alone.

Every now and then, I try to take us out to a night spot or to a party, but I always turn around and take us home before we arrive. Even though I've never gone, I always get invited to the parties. I am a living conversation piece carrying a dead one. But everywhere we go feels so crowded. I imagine if the body could talk, it would tell me it feels the same way. It would say, If we go out, we will only run into people. Or we will only end up standing in the corner of the room watching everyone else. Or worse.

The Sunlight Is So Bright

When I look out my window, there is a man on the sidewalk scraping mud off his shoes with a stick. He is really scraping hard. The flesh on his face jiggles when he scrapes. His face and clothes are splattered with mud flecks and sweat.

I do not have to scrape mud off the dead body's shoes. And I don't ever have to buy it new shoes since it never walks and never rips holes in its shoes or wears the tread down or outgrows them. And unlike a pet or live roommate, it never eats my food if I accidentally leave it out. It never takes the last cookie and then puts the empty box back in the cabinet. It never drinks all the milk, leaving me milkless when I have already poured a bowl of cereal, or plays loud music or television shows at night.

Now the man outside is knocking the shoes together. And now he is wiping them in the grass. And now he is grumbling. And now he is wiping them faster. And now he is tearing up little clumps of grass, he is wiping them so hard. And now, even after all of this, the mud is still not coming off.

And now the dead body slumps over on the couch, its head cocked in an uncomfortable-looking position.

Taste and See

I have not given the body its special liquid formula today or any other day for the last week. It began as an experiment. Just to see what would happen. Now the body smells terrible. Much worse than usual. Its hair is starting to fall out, and its skin is oozing a sticky oil. The oil makes it difficult to carry the body.

It has become so difficult to carry, we have not left the house for three days—we just sit across the room from each other and stare. Every now and then I get up to get a bowl of cereal. I keep thinking about the bottle of formula on the windowsill. I still have no idea what is in the formula or how it works. I only know that sometime before they died, my parents gave me a lifetime supply of it in unlabeled bottles.

Promise your mother and me right now that you won't ever taste the formula. That you'll only feed it to the body, my father had said.

Sometimes I wonder if the body would want to taste my cereal.

Or be the one who does the talking and wondering.

Or the carrying.

O Taste and See

The body is in no shape to go anywhere tonight, not even to the woods or for a drive. I put an end to the experiment. I fed the body its formula again. But now the body is only getting worse, no matter how much formula I feed it. I do not know what will happen to us now. I prop the body up in a chair and sit across from it. We face each other, and I say to the body:

You have been my every day for years. You are something like my skin, and I am something like yours. We are a film projector and a screen. A stage and the actor upon it. A fist and the blow it contains. A light passes through us both.

The dead body does not answer me, so I imagine its answers:

Our life will have to change soon. We spend so much time together. In the woods. The car. In this room in the blue television light. A voice passes right through our mind. We are a tall shadow pressed into the pavement. Into the walls.

And then we say:

Look through the dead body, and there is Alex with his aching limbs. He was a born shadowboxer, a real champ. A dead body withers to nothing but a long, sticky shadow. You've got the weight. I've got the reach. We're all alone, kid. It's just you and me.

But soon a new space will open between us. A third face. A face made of both our faces. I can feel it.

A shadow shines on the floor. The refrigerator hums and rattles. I go into the kitchen, and I bring back a bowl of cereal and the bottle of special formula. I sit down beside the body. I open its mouth and feed it a spoonful of cereal. I work the jaw and let the cereal slide down the body's throat. I imagine how happy the body must be—to finally try cereal after all these years.

It must be as happy as I am when I pour a spoonful of the special liquid formula. When I hold it up to my mouth. When I touch the tip of my tongue to the liquid to taste. When I put the spoonful of the special formula in my mouth and swallow. When I feel the sweetness drip down the back of my throat.

II. The Room

(The Voice)

□

Alex is alone in the middle of a small white room. Alex and nobody. He looks around the new space. At the top of the first wall, there is a small square window about the size of Alex's head. Its glass is very thick. On the second wall, there is a mouth-sized hole labeled TALKHOLE. On the third wall, there is a black cable with a flat disc about the size of an ear on its end labeled HEARPIECE. The fourth wall is completely blank. No door or window. Alex runs his hand along the wall. He presses his ear up against it. No sounds. He presses his face, then his entire body against the wall. Imagines pressing himself through the wall completely. He wonders what could be on the other side. Alex gets a funny feeling in his belly. He knocks on the blank wall. It sounds very thin and hollow. He tries to shout, Where am I, how did I get here, how do I get out, but his voice is small in the room. In his own body, it sounds distant, like a shout from far away. When he hears no answer, when nobody comes for him, Alex does not know what to do. He cannot see a way out. He sits on the floor and watches each of the walls for an opening. He waits.

□

Alex is alone in the middle of the room. On the floor, he finds a finger-sized piece of black chalk. He picks it up and turns it slowly in his hands. He takes the chalk over to the blank white wall and writes: WHAT IS THIS PLACE. HOW DID I GET HERE. THERE IS NO WAY IN OR OUT. I DON'T UNDERSTAND. SOMETHING IS MISSING. Alex thinks hard, but he cannot figure out what is missing. He draws a box on the wall. He fills the box with scribbles, and a small pile of chalk dust gathers on the floor. He remembers playing in a pile of dirt. He remembers drawing his name in dirt, remembers dirt all over his hands. Alex puts his hands in the chalk dust. He draws a stick figure in the dust. He draws a second stick figure draped over the first stick figure's back. He imagines the stick figures standing up and walking into the blank wall, into the box. He feels like there is a small empty space somewhere inside of himself, pressing outward. What could I be missing, he thinks.

□

Alex is alone in the middle of the room. The words he wrote, the pictures he drew are gone. The wall is blank again. On the floor, he finds a new piece of black chalk. He picks it up, rubs his finger around its nice sharp edge. He tosses the chalk from hand to hand as he walks around the room. To get a better sense of the space, Alex decides to measure the room with his body. He places his feet on one wall and lies as flat as he can. He marks the floor at the top of his head with the chalk. Then he places his feet on the mark and stretches out again. The room is small. It is approximately two Alexes wide by two Alexes long by two Alexes high. He thinks of the room he lived in when he was a boy. It was approximately three Alexes wide by three and a half Alexes long by two and a half Alexes high. Not much bigger than this room, but it seemed bigger at the time. Alex stretches his arms out as far as he can and he smiles. He has expanded.

□

Alex is alone in the middle of the room. The measuring lines he made on the floor are gone. So is the chalk. Alex walks over to the window. He tries to jump and look out. He jumps as high as he can, but when he looks at the window, he cannot see through it. The window pumps the light in, but it lets no light escape. Alex stops jumping. He puts his hands on his face, his arms. He can feel the light on his skin. It is like the light shines into him, through him. Alex imagines his shadow on the wall, but it does not appear. He looks everywhere for a shadow in the room. He looks under the hearpiece cable. He looks in all of the room's corners. He holds his hand up to the light, but no shadow appears on the wall. He looks under his feet. No shadows on any of the room's surfaces. The only shadows in the room are within the darkness of the talkhole. Within the black cable attached to the hearpiece. Within Alex's body.

Alex is alone in the middle of the room. On the floor he finds nothing. Alex picks up the hearpiece. It does not make any sounds. He stretches the cable from one end of the room to the other. He pulls the cable and pulls the cable but cannot find the end of it. He pulls out so much cable it entangles his body, and he lies down on the floor. He imagines there are train tracks under him. A distant rushing noise comes from the hearpiece. He imagines the noise is from a train coming toward him. At the last minute, he untangles himself from the cable and holds the hearpiece to his ear. From the other end of the line he hears a voice. A voice that cuts through a fog of static. The voice sends a series of words through the hearpiece: *lightligtryhtwallspoontch wasdktchchalkickth hearhcvnearspoonchalkpiecetchk chtliquidlightchalk*. A code, Alex thinks. Alex does not know what the code means, but he can feel its language pass through him. He listens to the voice. It is flat and garbled, but inside it is a kindness. It is like the voice is there just for him. He listens to the voice for an hour or more. He wants to press the hearpiece all the way into his brain so the sound can resonate through his whole body, fill the space inside him. He looks at all the cable unspooled at his feet. He crawls under the cable and wraps himself in it. He pulls the hearpiece close and listens.

□

Alex is alone in the middle of the room. The cable has retracted back into the wall, and the hearpiece is silent again. Alex inspects the talkhole more closely. He looks as far down the talkhole as he can, but he cannot see anything in it but darkness. He puts his finger into the hole but cannot feel anything inside. No microphone, no wire, nothing. It is just a hole. Alex tries to think of something to say into the hole. He clears his throat, takes a breath and says loudly, Hello. His voice rings and rings in the talkhole like a feedback loop. Like the word has reached into a void. His word expands in the void and projects back into the room. He lets the word decay while he decides what to say next. He speaks from deep within himself when he says, in a quieter voice, What is the voice that spoke to me through the hearpiece. Can I hear the voice again. I just want to hear the voice again. He repeats these words over and over until his throat is so sore he can no longer speak.

□

Alex is alone in the middle of the room. The hearpiece is silent, and his throat is sore. On the floor he finds nothing. Alex walks around the room. He is bored. There is nothing to do. He goes over to the talkhole but gets too nervous to speak into it. What if he seemed too needy before when he pled to know what the voice was, to hear the voice again. What if the voice wasn't real, if it was just some old recording of a voice that has been dead for some time now. Or what if the voice was real and alive and something terrible happened to its owner. He imagines a disembodied voice short-circuiting in the hearpiece. He imagines the voice strangled in the wires. He imagines the voice's owner stuck in the cable, unable to call for help. What if the voice does not come back, he thinks. Alex paces the room. His thoughts clump. He feels the need to lift something heavy. He wishes he had a boxing partner. He wishes he had a bowl of cereal and someone to share it with.

Someone to talk to. Someone to tell him everything will be alright.

A companion.

□

Alex is alone in the middle of the room. He checks the hearpiece: still silent. Still his throat feels raw. A thick liquid begins to flow from the talkhole, stains a path down the wall, and puddles on the floor. Alex looks up and down the line of the stain. The talkhole must be broken, he thinks. He imagines the liquid is a trail of ants that have chewed up the talkhole's electrical lines, their bellies full of sparks. The liquid glimmers down the wall. Alex dabs at the liquid with his finger. It is sticky. He imagines the liquid dripping out of his body, imagines being covered by it. He touches his finger to his tongue and tastes the liquid. It is sweet and thick. Perhaps the talkhole is also a foodhole, but without a label. He licks the liquid off his finger. He stoops and licks up the puddle on the floor, licks up and down the wall. The talkhole glubs out more and more of the liquid. Someone on the other side is paying attention to him. Alex puts his mouth to the talkhole. He feeds.

□

Alex is alone in the middle of the room. The hearpiece is silent and the talkhole is dry. On the floor he finds nothing. He stares at the walls. He stays very still and listens for the voice to come from the hearpiece, but there is no sound. He wonders if the voice is watching him. When he gets tired of waiting, of staring at the window, the talkhole, the hearpiece, the blank wall, Alex trots laps around the room. There is no weight to hold him down, only walls to hold him in, the smallness of the room. But in the moment when he heard the voice, Alex felt a space inside himself expand. Soon, he thinks, the voice will return. Soon the room will not be able to contain their space.

□

Alex is alone in the middle of the room. He says *hello* into the talkhole. The hearpiece is silent. He says *hello* again, but still gets no answer. On the floor he finds a new piece of black chalk. He draws an outline of himself on the blank wall. His shadow. He colors it in with black chalk. The shadow raises a pair of fists. Alex has a new boxing partner. Alex bounces around the room with his shoulders hunched. He bobs and weaves. He puts up his dukes. He jabs, hooks, crosses. Even in this small space, he thinks, my moves are really good. He hopes the voice is watching him. He imagines the voice on a loudspeaker saying, *And in this corner, measuring in at approximately one Alex and expanding the room with his presence, please welcome the champ into the ring: Aaaa-leeeeex.* Alex and the shadow touch fists, then take their stances. The bell rings. The crowd goes wild.

□

Alex is alone in the middle of the room. He hears a tiny noise coming from the hearpiece again, and he runs over to pick it up. *...me can you hear me can you hear me can you*, the voice says. Yes, Alex says, dragging the hearpiece over to the talkhole, I can hear you, I'm here, I can hear you. *Hello*, the voice whispers. *I have been watching you.* I knew it was you, watching, sending me things, Alex says. Even in the silence, I could feel your voice in the room. Ringing in my body. *Are you hungry still.*

□

Alex is alone in the middle of the room. On the floor in front of him is a spoon. He picks up the spoon and puts it in his mouth. It dissolves. It is sweet, the most delicious spoon he has ever tasted. Like a combo of cereal and a sweet syrup. Alex feels strong, bold. His thoughts unclump. He goes to the talkhole and says, Thank you for the spoon. It's delicious. He picks up the hearpiece and, still licking the spoon, waits for a reply. Soon the voice comes. *I am sorry I could not get a bowl of cereal for you. The room is a strange place. I still do not understand it. There are only certain things I can send you. Certain items that can pass into the room.* Can you enter the room, Alex says. *Only my voice. Only my words.* Are you also alone. *No. There are others here.* What others. *Other faces. Other voices. Others.* Through the hearpiece, Alex hears a distant applause. Then there is a long pause. Alex hears the voice gather a question. *Alex, tell me, what do you want. Tell us what you want.*

Um. *Please. We—I want to know you.* Alex clears his throat and looks at the floor. He thinks about leaving the room. He thinks about opening the window, about pressing his body through the blank wall. He thinks about being near the voice, hearing the voice, speaking to the voice. His thoughts clump in his head again, and he is unable to speak. Alex moves closer to the talkhole, closer still, puts his hand on the wall, presses his mouth against the talkhole. As he begins to speak, he imagines his voice approaching the void.

□

Alex and the voice talk until they are too hoarse to continue. Then Alex just stands there and breathes into the talkhole. He listens to the voice breathe. Alex breathes. The voice breathes. Alex. The voice. Alex. The voice. The voice. The voice.

□

Can you see me—right now, Alex says into the talkhole. He holds the hearpiece close. *Everyone here can see you*, the voice says. *We watch you through the walls. Watch you run laps around the room. Watch you shadowbox. Watch you feed on spoons and liquid and draw with chalk and tangle yourself in the hearpiece cable.* Alex looks around the room. He tries to see through the walls, but there is only the blankness. He almost smiles. He touches his face. He says, Do you know what is happening to me. *I do not.* Do you know why I am in this room. *I do not.* It's so lonely in here. *I will send words.* How do I get out. *There is no out. Only a different space. An absence. A space within a void.* What do I do, Alex says. How do I go into a different space. *You have to use everything.*

□

The room is different. Alex can feel it. He is still alone. The hearpiece is silent. The talkhole is dry. On the floor he finds nothing. It is the window that has changed, the light. Alex rushes over to the window. He leaps and looks through, and when he looks through, some of the light is torn from his eyes, and for an instant he can see for miles and miles into a deep shadow that expands as his vision passes through it, expands into another place filled with shadows, a host of shadows that get closer and closer, and he can feel them but he cannot see their faces, and he hears them laugh, he hears them *ooh* and *ahh*, and then they begin to shrink, and his vision rides the little bit of light, the light that leaks through the window, back into his body, and Alex falls to the floor. He cannot breathe. He cannot think. A shiver shoots through his spine. He imagines the voice filling his head. Imagines holding a piece of chalk, then breaking the chalk, grinding it to powder, watching it blow away. Alex imagines a bowl and spoon. He imagines tapping the spoon on the rim of the bowl until the bowl shatters. Alex feels the sound in his teeth. He hears it. He realizes the tapping sound is coming from the hearpiece. He scrambles over to it, but when he holds it to his ear, he first hears nothing but static, then the tapping, then a hum. Under the hum, Alex can barely make out the sound of the voice. It is small and far away. He cannot understand any of its words. The voice sounds farther and farther away until, finally, he can hear only the static, the tapping, the hum. Then just the static and the tapping. Then just the static.

□

Alex hurls his body into each of the walls, from wall to wall, again and again. He begins to bruise. His shoulders ache. The weight has returned. He knows the voice is gone. Knows it has been taken away. Knows he cannot stay in the room without the voice. He screams into the talkhole: What did you do with the voice. What are you doing to me. To us. What do you want. Then he doubles over. He cannot catch his breath. He presses his hands to a pain as it grows in his head. The space of the room has collapsed into itself, into Alex. It feels larger and smaller at the same time. Alex presses against the wall to lift himself back to the talkhole again. He says, Is there still someone watching me. He crawls over to the hearpiece and cradles it to his ear. Static. Static. Static. The light grows brighter. Alex drops the hearpiece. He is alone in the middle of the room. On the floor Alex finds a new piece of black chalk and a spoon. When he picks them up, the talkhole begins to gush.

Alex looks at the chalk and spoon in his hands, then at the liquid gushing from the talkhole, then at the blank wall.

□

Alex stands alone in the middle of the room, the spoon and chalk gripped tightly in his hand, the talkhole gushing, the pain in his head droning, the light blaring. He uses the chalk to write I AM COMING THROUGH NOW at the top of the blank wall. He scoops up some of the chalk's dust and mixes it with the talkhole's special liquid. He dips the spoon into the mixture and spreads the mixture all over the blank wall in the shape of an Alex shadow. He bobs and weaves around the room. Does all of his moves. He takes the hearpiece in his hand. He pulls as much of its cable from the walls as he can and he tracks it around the room. He makes a new space with the cable. He makes a new space with the chalk dust liquid formula mixture and the spoon. He makes a new space with his words on the wall. He puts up his dukes. He approaches the shadow he drew on the wall. The shadow has sunk into the wall. Near the shadow's head, the wall has grown thinner. He throws a jab into the thinnest part of the wall. A hook. A cross. As he delivers the blows, he says to the others who watch him through the wall: Here is everything: my spoon, my chalk, my liquid, my moves, my shadow, my space, my love, my voice, my voice, my voice, my face, my body, my void. Now do you see me now do you see me do you see who I am do you love watching me and do you love me do you love me do you

□

When Alex breaks open a hole in the wall, another hole throbs open in his head, not enough to hurt or kill him, just enough to let smoke drift from the hole in his head and into the empty room. Alex exhales and watches the smoke fill the room. He goes to the wall, presses his head to the hole he made, and lets his smoke drift through. In that space, Alex hears the voice grow clear and close. Then comes the faint sound of applause.

III. The Smoke

(The Stage)

((The Star))

■

Alex emerges from the hole in the wall. From his head, a smoke cloud spreads. The smoke shrouds the new space in mystery. Alex coughs and waves the smoke away with his hand. He is on a dark stage. He can hear the floorboards creak beneath his weight. Glass clinking, scuffling sounds, hushed voices. From the back of the space, a spotlight cuts through the smoke and shines onto Alex, right into his face. The light shines into some deep place inside of him. The light holds Alex, and he feels strange, like he is no longer in control of his own body. He feels his hands rise in front of his face. They turn and flex in the light. He looks at them. The light saturates his skin, and he can feel its heat, but it is a distant feeling. The audience applauds, and Alex looks into the thick smear of black. He cannot see anything beyond the blare of the spotlight. Alex feels his feet take a few steps forward, and when his feet find the edge of the stage, he hears the audience gasp. He looks up.

The spotlight refracts in the smoke from his head. His feet take a step back from the edge, and then they do a little soft-shoe. The audience laughs and applauds. Alex looks out into the dark field beyond the stage. He feels the eyes of the audience upon him. His skin glows. The smoke billows from his head hole. Alex feels his body bow, then he hears his own voice say, Well that's all for tonight folks. You've been a wonderful audience. His voice sounds strange to him, like it comes from a place beyond himself. He does not know where the words came from, does not remember sending them through his voice. Alex is deep inside of his own body. He feels his body move toward the curtain.

■

Behind the curtain, Alex feels the light release his body. He feels weak. Emptied. Like so much energy has been pulled through his face, his face stretched, worn out. Slowly Alex shuffles down the dark hallway backstage. The hallway echoes. It is a deep black throat. Alex imagines how his voice would sound ringing through the hallway. Hello, he says. When he speaks, it is not with the voice that came through him onstage. In the hallway his voice is raspy and small. Is there anybody here. Can anybody hear me. He sees nobody. Hears no voice beyond his own. At the end of the hallway is a door labeled GREENROOM. Alex opens the door, stumbles in, and lets his body slump onto the couch just inside. Without the spotlight to hold him, without the audience watching, laughing, applauding, Alex feels hollow, his body nothing but an empty, ringing room.

■

Alex curls into a ball on the couch, reaches up, feels the hole in his head. The smoke exits his headhole in gentle wisps. He presses his cheek into the cushion and stares blankly across the room. The greenroom is empty except for a large circular clothes rack and a wall mirror. Something about the rack of clothes is strange. Alex rises from the couch and looks at it more closely. He flips through a few items, then stops. The rack is full of ALEX costumes, each of them identical. Identical ALEX skins. Identical ALEX faces.

■

One by one, Alex takes each ALEX costume from the rack and holds it up to the mirror on the wall. They aren't just good copies of Alex—each costume is an exact replica. The same mess of brown hair, same eye and mouth holes, same plaid button-up shirt and blue jeans. The same pale skin and thin frame, only formless, waiting to be filled by a body. Attached to the sleeve of each ALEX is a tag. He reads them aloud:

LONER / LOVER / PERFORMER / SURVEILLANT / VAGRANT
RASCAL / WATCHER / PARTICLE / FRAGMENT / PROPHET
TEACHER / HERO / VILLAIN / FOIL / WALLFLOWER / ORPHAN
SON / DAUGHTER / FATHER / MOTHER / BROTHER / SISTER / MAN
BOY / WOMAN / GIRL / CHILD / CITIZEN / LOYALIST / THIEF
FUTURE / OBJECT / SUBJECT / DEFORMER / FORMER / CHEATER
COWARD / BELIEVER / DOUBTER / RADICAL / HYSTERIC / ALIEN

KILLER / VICTIM / REJECT / UNKNOWN / CELEBRITY / INFAMOUS

ADORED / IGNORED / HEAVY-LADEN / LIGHTENED / ENLIGHTENED

IDIOT / SHADOWBOXER / CARRIER / PRISONER / POSEUR / “REAL”

LOSER / VICTOR / SMOKER / SHADOW / HOLE / LACERATION

DEAD / BODY / SPACE / VOICE / VOID / VOID / VOID / VOID / VOID

/ /

/ /

///

■

Alex takes off his clothes and puts on an ALEX costume labeled STAR. When he looks into the mirror he appears to be slightly larger, like his presence has pushed outward, expanded. At the same time, he feels how the costume gathers even the dimmest light in the greenroom into his body. The energy. The smoke comes out of his head in thick plumes. He feels more like Alex than he has ever felt before.

■

Alex gathers all of the ALEX costumes and carries them into the dark theater space. He drapes an ALEX costume onto each seat. He moves quickly. He leaves a smoke trail as he rushes up and down and through the aisles. When all of the ALEX costumes have been placed, he lifts himself onto the stage and hides behind the curtain. He waits for the spotlight to come, for the audience to arrive.

■

The space fills with bodies. From behind the curtain, Alex watches as the audience members try on their ALEX costumes. Alexes unfold the seats and sit down. Alexes carry large buckets of popcorn. Alexes sip drinks through straws. Alexes hold hands with other Alexes. Alexes feed bottles to smaller Alexes. Alexes murmur as showtime approaches. The entire theater is full of Alex. Backstage, Alex fidgets with the curtain. His leg shakes. His eyes are bright. He does a little dance backstage. He listens to the floorboards squeak. The smoke leaves his head in little excited puffs.

■

When the spotlight switches on, it pulls Alex from behind the curtain. Pulls him to the middle of the stage. Grips him. Holds him there. The audience applauds. Alex feels his body move in the light. His arms rise over his head in a welcome gesture. He feels his throat open. GOOD EVENING AUDIENCE, it says through his on-stage voice. The audience applauds. The applause is deafening. Alex feels his entire body ring with the sound.

■

FOR THE FIRST SEGMENT OF THE EVENING I NEED AN ALEX FROM THE AUDIENCE, Alex says. From the back of the space, an audience member wearing a DEAD ALEX costume tumbles down the stairs and thunks against the foot of the stage. Alex pulls the dead Alex onto the stage and hoists him onto his back. The audience claps a little. The chairs squeak as they lean forward in their seats. Just stay dead, Alex whispers to the dead Alex slung motionless over his shoulders. With exaggerated movements, Alex walks back and forth across the stage carrying the body. Props the body up against the wall, stage right. Mimes cleaning and feeding the body. Finally he lays the body flat on the stage then lies down beside it. Cheers erupt throughout the space. Whoops and hollers. A tide of applause crashes and rolls across the stage. The smoke from Alex's head shimmers in the spotlight. Alex stands and takes a bow.

■

There are many segments in the evening. In one segment, Alex makes chalk drawings on a white screen that drops onto the stage. The audience is impressed by his shapes, his figures. They make *ooh* and *ahh* noises with each line he draws. Alex takes a bow. In another segment, Alex shadowboxes with a costumed shadow-boxer Alex all around the stage. The audience gasps at the quickness of his jabs, the power in his uppercut, the deftness of his feet as he moves around the space. They cheer and cheer. Alex begins to feel the grip of the spotlight relax around him. In another segment Alex pretends to be trapped in a box of wallflower Alexes. He hugs his body to make it appear small and trapped. He mimes talking to someone over a great distance. Finally he mimes breaking through the wallflower Alexes and crawls through to the other side. After so much time onstage, Alex cannot tell the difference between his moves and the moves the spotlight sends through him.

His moves and those of the other Alexes. Alex, he thinks. Where is Alex. He breathes heavily. He wipes sweat from his brow. He takes a bow and says, THANK YOU THANK YOU FOLKS THAT'S ALL FOR TONIGHT YOU'VE BEEN A GREAT AUDIENCE. He bows and waves to the audience, but they do not move from their seats. The audience begins clapping. Stomping in unison. Their voices join together. Stack upon each other. Grow larger. They chant, *More, more, more, more*, over and over again. Alex stands at the end of the stage and tries to smile. I'm sorry folks, he says, his voice far away. I'm afraid the evening is over. I don't have anything left to give you. Goodnight. Alex's head rings with *more, more, more, more*. From the blackness, Alex sees a flash of silver fly toward him. It strikes his face and lands at his feet: a metal spoon. Alex retreats to the back of the stage, but the spotlight tightens its grip on him again. It will not let him leave. *Make us feel another thing*, the audience commands. Alex freezes. He looks desperately into the spotlight. The spotlight glares into his face. Steadily. From the audience, another object flies onto the stage. It lands at the lip and rolls across the stage until it comes to a rest against Alex's foot. A plastic bottle full of a thick liquid. *Eat it, eat it, eat it, eat it*, they chant. Alex stares at the bottle. The smoke from his head is thick and black. He picks up the bottle and unscrews the cap. The room falls silent. Alex feels a burn behind his cheeks. His feels the shame clot in the redness of his cheeks. He smiles weakly at the audience, but the smile almost collapses into tears. Alex pours a spoonful of the liquid and puts it in his mouth. He swallows. His lips tremble. The audience roars.

■

As the audience continues to applaud, the spotlight releases Alex. It glares onto his face, but it does not move through him. Alex drops the spoon and bottle of liquid. Slowly he takes off the STAR ALEX costume and stands at the edge of the stage. Now he is nothing but regular Alex. Sweat pours down his face. Smoke sprays from his headhole. His eyes are wide. Look at me, Alex says into the darkness of the theater. I want you to see me. See me, not star Alex. Look at the hole in my head, the smoke that rises from it. Look at the light on my face, at the shadows that gather on my body. Look at how my body moves, how my shoulders handle the weight of other bodies, how my body expands, how it fills the bare stage. Listen to how my body is full of voice. Listen to how it rings. Look at how my body is so often held by the spotlight, how it is propped up by your attention, how you project yourselves onto me, into me. This is a body that would collapse without you.

Without you, this body is another Alex costume. See. Alex looks into the darkness of the audience. All I have ever wanted is to see someone. For someone to see me. For us to see each other and not turn away.

■

The theater is silent. The smoke from Alex's head sputters, then stops. All of the Alexes face him. They wait. Alex feels their eyes on his skin. Their eyes stab into him, bore into him. Alex quivers. This is not what he wanted. It is worse than the hollow feeling he had in the greenroom. He tries to hide his face with his hands. He feels his skin burn in the stares, in the spotlight. No, he shouts, not like that. The spotlight glares at him. The spotlight glares into him. The spotlight glares into him and grows hotter, grows hotter. Alex picks up the spoon from the stage, picks up the spoon and raises it high over his head, throws the spoon out into the blackness of the theater. It sails up, up, over the heads of the audience, over the dark chairscape, up, past each row, past a thousand audience members each wearing an ALEX costume, up all the way to the back of the room. Where it hits the spotlight. Shatters the spotlight. Destroys the spotlight and the spotlight explodes and the light darkens. The audience applauds. They stand and clap and cheer for several minutes. Then Alex hears the audience members slip off their ALEX costumes and file out of the theater.

■

Alex is alone in the center of the stage. The stage is black and cold. Alex looks out at the empty rows and aisles, the empty seats, the empty ALEX costumes draped over each one. Alex is empty. He picks up the STAR ALEX costume, drapes it over his shoulder and drags his own body through the curtain. Backstage. Down the hallway. Back into the greenroom.

■

When Alex enters the greenroom dragging the STAR ALEX costume, there is something waiting for him on the couch. A face. It is a kind face. Something about the face reminds him of the voice in the room. He puts his hand on the face. It is smooth and warm, alive. Touching the face spreads a soft glow through Alex. He picks up the face. There is a voice machine behind the face. Alex presses its PLAY button, and from the face comes the sound of the voice. *Alex*, it says, *when you get tired of looking only at yourselves, of being looked at only by yourselves, here is my face. We can look into each other.* The voice machine stops. Alex lets the STAR ALEX costume fall at his feet, and he holds the face gently with both hands. He closes his eyes and holds the face up to his own. He touches his nose to its nose, his mouth to its mouth. He breathes through the face, and when he does, the face breathes through him. Alex opens his eyes and looks into the eyes of the face. The face looks back.

The look from the face does not bore painfully into him. The look is not a burn on his skin. It does not grip him like a spotlight. The smoke stops drifting from his headhole. Alex and the face stand there like that. Seeing. They see each other, and the face does not flinch. The face does not turn away.

■

Neither does Alex.

Thanks to Amanda Raczkowski and Joseph Reed for your patience and sharp editing; to the Creative Writing Program at the University of Minnesota; to Alexs Pate and the Fall 2011 Fiction Workshop, especially Jonathan Escoffery, Rose Hansen, Isabel Harding, C. Joseph Jordan, Zoë Miller, and Adriane Quinlan; to Sarah Fox, Lucas de Lima, and David Malley for many things beyond the text; to Angharad Davies for the stage experience; to MH Rowe for reading, pacing floors, and other feats of strength; to Austin Grant, who has and will run far; and, of course, to Randy and Shirley Grant for being wonderful and supportive parents who have only given me good gifts.

A.T. Grant lives in Virginia, where people call him Alex.

CPSIA information can be obtained at www.ICGtesting.com
Printed in the USA
LVOW12s0252110713

342378LV00001B/9/P